In the Year 2889

In the Year 2889
Jules Verne and
Michel Verne

MINT EDITIONS

In the Year 2889 was first published in 1889.

This edition published by Mint Editions 2021.

ISBN 9781513269863 | E-ISBN 9781513274867

Published by Mint Editions®

 MINT
EDITIONS

minteditionbooks.com

Publishing Director: Jennifer Newens
Design & Production: Rachel Lopez Metzger
Project Manager: Micaela Clark
Typesetting: Westchester Publishing Services

Little though they seem to think of it, the people of this twenty-ninth century live continually in fairyland. Surfeited as they are with marvels, they are indifferent in presence of each new marvel. To them all seems natural. Could they but duly appreciate the refinements of civilization in our day; could they but compare the present with the past, and so better comprehend the advance we have made! How much fairer they would find our modern towns, with populations amounting sometimes to 10,000,000 souls; their streets 300 feet wide, their houses 1000 feet in height; with a temperature the same in all seasons; with their lines of aërial locomotion crossing the sky in every direction! If they would but picture to themselves the state of things that once existed, when through muddy streets rumbling boxes on wheels, drawn by horses—yes, by horses!—were the only means of conveyance. Think of the railroads of the olden time, and you will be able to appreciate the pneumatic tubes through which to-day one travels at the rate of 1000 miles an hour. Would not our contemporaries prize the telephone and the telephote more highly if they had not forgotten the telegraph?

Singularly enough, all these transformations rest upon principles which were perfectly familiar to our remote ancestors, but which they disregarded. Heat, for instance, is as ancient as man himself; electricity was known 3000 years ago, and steam 1100 years ago. Nay, so early as ten centuries ago it was known that the differences between the several chemical and physical forces depend on the mode of vibration of the etheric particles, which is for each specifically different. When at last the kinship of all these forces was discovered, it is simply astounding that 500 years should still have to elapse before men could analyze and describe the several modes of vibration that constitute these differences. Above all, it is singular that the mode of reproducing these forces directly from one another, and of reproducing one without the others, should have remained undiscovered till less than a hundred years ago. Nevertheless, such was the course of events, for it was not till the year 2792 that the famous Oswald Nier made this great discovery.

Truly was he a great benefactor of the human race. His admirable discovery led to many another. Hence is sprung a pleiad of inventors, its brightest star being our great Joseph Jackson. To Jackson we are indebted for those wonderful instruments the new accumulators. Some of these absorb and condense the living force contained in the sun's rays; others, the electricity stored in our globe; others again, the energy coming from whatever source, as a waterfall, a stream, the winds, etc. He, too, it was that invented the transformer, a more wonderful contrivance still, which takes the living force from the accumulator, and, on the simple pressure of a button, gives it back to space in whatever form may be desired, whether as heat, light, electricity, or mechanical force, after having first obtained from it the work required. From the day when these two instruments were contrived is to be dated the era of true progress. They have put into the hands of man a power that is almost infinite. As for their applications, they are numberless. Mitigating the rigors of winter, by giving back to the atmosphere the surplus heat stored up during the summer, they have revolutionized agriculture. By supplying motive power for aërial navigation, they have given to commerce a mighty impetus. To them we are indebted for the continuous production of electricity without batteries or dynamos, of light without combustion or incandescence, and for an unfailing supply of mechanical energy for all the needs of industry.

Yes, all these wonders have been wrought by the accumulator and the transformer. And can we not to them also trace, indirectly, this latest wonder of all, the great "Earth Chronicle" building in 253d Avenue, which was dedicated the other day? If George Washington Smith, the founder of the Manhattan "Chronicle," should come back to life to-day, what would he think were he to be told that this palace of marble and gold belongs to his remote descendant, Fritz Napoleon Smith, who, after thirty generations have come and gone, is owner of the same newspaper which his ancestor established!

For George Washington Smith's newspaper has lived generation after generation, now passing out of the family, anon coming back to it. When, 200 years ago, the political center of the United States was transferred from Washington to Centropolis, the newspaper followed the government and assumed the name of Earth Chronicle. Unfortunately, it was unable to maintain itself at the high level of its name. Pressed on all sides by rival journals of a more modern type, it was continually in danger of collapse. Twenty years ago its subscription list contained but a few hundred thousand names, and then Mr. Fritz Napoleon Smith bought it for a mere trifle, and originated telephonic journalism.

Every one is familiar with Fritz Napoleon Smith's system—a system made possible by the enormous development of telephony during the last hundred years. Instead of being printed, the Earth Chronicle is every morning spoken to subscribers, who, in interesting conversations with reporters, statesmen, and scientists, learn the news of the day.

Furthermore, each subscriber owns a phonograph, and to this instrument he leaves the task of gathering the news whenever he happens not to be in a mood to listen directly himself. As for purchasers of single copies, they can at a very trifling cost learn all that is in the paper of the day at any of the innumerable phonographs set up nearly everywhere.

Fritz Napoleon Smith's innovation galvanized the old newspaper. In the course of a few years the number of subscribers grew to be 85,000,000, and Smith's wealth went on growing, till now it reaches the almost unimaginable figure of $10,000,000,000. This lucky hit has enabled him to erect his new building, a vast edifice with four *façades*, each 3,250 feet in length, over which proudly floats the hundred-starred flag of the Union. Thanks to the same lucky hit, he is to-day king of newspaperdom; indeed, he would be king of all the Americans, too, if Americans could ever accept a king. You do not believe it? Well, then, look at the plenipotentiaries of all nations and our own ministers themselves crowding about his door, entreating his counsels, begging for his approbation, imploring the aid of his all-powerful organ. Reckon up the number of scientists and artists that he supports, of inventors that he has under his pay.

Yes, a king is he. And in truth his is a royalty full of burdens. His labors are incessant, and there is no doubt at all that in earlier times any man would have succumbed under the overpowering stress of the toil which Mr. Smith has to perform. Very fortunately for him, thanks to the progress of hygiene, which, abating all the old sources of unhealthfulness, has lifted the mean of human life from 37 up to 52 years, men have stronger constitutions now than heretofore. The discovery of nutritive air is still in the future, but in the meantime men today consume food that is compounded and prepared according to scientific principles, and they breathe an atmosphere freed from the micro-organisms that formerly used to swarm in it; hence they live longer than their forefathers and know nothing of the innumerable diseases of olden times.

Nevertheless, and notwithstanding these considerations, Fritz Napoleon Smith's mode of life may well astonish one. His iron constitution is taxed to the utmost by the heavy strain that is put upon it. Vain the attempt to estimate the amount of labor he undergoes; an example alone can give an idea of it. Let us then go about with him for one day as he attends to his multifarious concernments. What day? That matters little; it is the same every day. Let us then take at random September 25th of this present year 2889.

This morning Mr. Fritz Napoleon Smith awoke in very bad humor. His wife having left for France eight days ago, he was feeling disconsolate. Incredible though it seems, in all the ten years since their marriage, this is the first time that Mrs. Edith Smith, the professional beauty, has been so long absent from home; two or three days usually suffice for her frequent trips to Europe. The first thing that Mr. Smith does is to connect his phonotelephote, the wires of which communicate with his Paris mansion. The telephote! Here is another of the great triumphs of science in our time. The transmission of speech is an old story; the transmission of images by means of sensitive mirrors connected by wires is a thing but of yesterday. A valuable invention indeed, and Mr. Smith this morning was not niggard of blessings for the inventor, when by its aid he was able distinctly to see his wife notwithstanding the distance that separated him from her. Mrs. Smith, weary after the ball or the visit to the theater the preceding night, is still abed, though it is near noontide at Paris. She is asleep, her head sunk in the lace-covered pillows. What? She stirs? Her lips move. She is dreaming perhaps? Yes, dreaming. She is talking, pronouncing a name—his name—Fritz! The delightful vision gave a happier turn to Mr. Smith's thoughts. And now, at the call of imperative duty, light-hearted he springs from his bed and enters his mechanical dresser.

Two minutes later the machine deposited him all dressed at the threshold of his office. The round of journalistic work was now begun. First he enters the hall of the novel-writers, a vast apartment crowned with an enormous transparent cupola. In one corner is a telephone, through which a hundred Earth Chronicle *littérateurs* in turn recount to the public in daily installments a hundred novels. Addressing one of these authors who was waiting his turn, "Capital! Capital! my dear fellow," said he, "your last story. The scene where the village maid discusses interesting philosophical problems with her lover shows your very acute power of observation. Never have the ways of country folk been better portrayed. Keep on, my dear Archibald, keep on! Since yesterday, thanks to you, there is a gain of 5000 subscribers."

"Mr. John Last," he began again, turning to a new arrival, "I am not so well pleased with your work. Your story is not a picture of life; it lacks the elements of truth. And why? Simply because you run straight on to the end; because you do not analyze. Your heroes do this thing or that from this or that motive, which you assign without ever a thought of dissecting their mental and moral natures. Our feelings, you must remember, are far more complex than all that. In real life every act is the resultant of a hundred thoughts that come and go, and these you must study, each by itself, if you would create a living character. 'But,' you will say, 'in order to note these fleeting thoughts one must know them, must be able to follow them in their capricious meanderings.' Why, any child can do that, as you know. You have simply to make use of hypnotism, electrical or human, which gives one a two-fold being, setting free the witness-personality so that it may see, understand, and remember the reasons which determine the personality that acts. Just study yourself as you live from day to day, my dear Last. Imitate your associate whom I was complimenting a moment ago. Let yourself be hypnotized. What's that? You have tried it already? Not sufficiently, then, not sufficiently!"

Mr. Smith continues his round and enters the reporters' hall. Here 1500 reporters, in their respective places, facing an equal number of telephones, are communicating to the subscribers the news of the world as gathered during the night. The organization of this matchless service has often been described. Besides his telephone, each reporter, as the reader is aware, has in front of him a set of commutators, which enable him to communicate with any desired telephotic line. Thus the subscribers not only hear the news but see the occurrences. When an incident is described that is already past, photographs of its main features are transmitted with the narrative. And there is no confusion withal. The reporters' items, just like the different stories and all the other component parts of the journal, are classified automatically according to an ingenious system, and reach the hearer in due succession. Furthermore, the hearers are free to listen only to what specially concerns them. They may at pleasure give attention to one editor and refuse it to another.

Mr. Smith next addresses one of the ten reporters in the astronomical department—a department still in the embryonic stage, but which will yet play an important part in journalism.

"Well, Cash, what's the news?"

"We have phototelegrams from Mercury, Venus, and Mars."

"Are those from Mars of any interest?"

"Yes, indeed. There is a revolution in the Central Empire."

"And what of Jupiter?" asked Mr. Smith.

"Nothing as yet. We cannot quite understand their signals. Perhaps ours do not reach them."

"That's bad," exclaimed Mr. Smith, as he hurried away, not in the best of humor, toward the hall of the scientific editors. With their heads bent down over their electric computers, thirty scientific men were absorbed in transcendental calculations. The coming of Mr. Smith was like the falling of a bomb among them.

"Well, gentlemen, what is this I hear? No answer from Jupiter? Is it always to be thus? Come, Cooley, you have been at work now twenty years on this problem, and yet—"

"True enough," replied the man addressed. "Our science of optics is still very defective, and through our mile-and-three-quarter telescopes—"

"Listen to that, Peer," broke in Mr. Smith, turning to a second scientist. "Optical science defective! Optical science is your specialty. But," he continued, again addressing William Cooley, "failing with Jupiter, are we getting any results from the moon?"

"The case is no better there."

"This time you do not lay the blame on the science of optics. The moon is immeasurably less distant than Mars, yet with Mars our communication is fully established. I presume you will not say that you lack telescopes?"

"Telescopes? O no, the trouble here is about—inhabitants!"

"That's it," added Peer.

"So, then, the moon is positively uninhabited?" asked Mr. Smith.

"At least," answered Cooley, "on the face which she presents to us. As for the opposite side, who knows?"

"Ah, the opposite side! You think, then," remarked Mr. Smith, musingly, "that if one could but—"

"Could what?"

"Why, turn the moon about-face."

"Ah, there's something in that," cried the two men at once. And indeed, so confident was their air, they seemed to have no doubt as to the possibility of success in such an undertaking.

"Meanwhile," asked Mr. Smith, after a moment's silence, "have you no news of interest to-day?"

"Indeed we have," answered Cooley. "The elements of Olympus are definitively settled. That great planet gravitates beyond Neptune at the mean distance of 11,400,799,642 miles from the sun, and to traverse its vast orbit takes 1311 years, 294 days, 12 hours, 43 minutes, 9 seconds."

"Why didn't you tell me that sooner?" cried Mr. Smith. "Now inform the reporters of this straightway. You know how eager is the curiosity of the public with regard to these astronomical questions. That news must go into to-day's issue."

Then, the two men bowing to him, Mr. Smith passed into the next hall, an enormous gallery upward of 3200 feet in length, devoted to atmospheric advertising. Every one has noticed those enormous advertisements reflected from the clouds, so large that they may be seen by the populations of whole cities or even of entire countries. This, too, is one of Mr. Fritz Napoleon Smith's ideas, and in the Earth Chronicle building a thousand projectors are constantly engaged in displaying upon the clouds these mammoth advertisements.

When Mr. Smith to-day entered the sky-advertising department, he found the operators sitting with folded arms at their motionless projectors, and inquired as to the cause of their inaction. In response, the man addressed simply pointed to the sky, which was of a pure blue. "Yes," muttered Mr. Smith, "a cloudless sky! That's too bad, but what's to be done? Shall we produce rain? That we might do, but is it of any use? What we need is clouds, not rain. Go," said he, addressing the head engineer, "go see Mr. Samuel Mark, of the meteorological division of the scientific department, and tell him for me to go to work in earnest on the question of artificial clouds. It will never do for us to be always thus at the mercy of cloudless skies!"

Mr. Smith's daily tour through the several departments of his newspaper is now finished. Next, from the advertisement hall he passes to the reception chamber, where the ambassadors accredited to the American government are awaiting him, desirous of having a word of counsel or advice from the all-powerful editor. A discussion was going on when he entered. "Your Excellency will pardon me," the French Ambassador was saying to the Russian, "but I see nothing in the map of Europe that requires change. 'The North for the Slavs?' Why, yes, of course; but the South for the Latins. Our common frontier, the Rhine, it seems to me, serves very well. Besides, my government, as you must know, will firmly oppose every movement, not only against Paris, our capital, or our two great prefectures, Rome and Madrid, but also against the kingdom of Jerusalem, the dominion of Saint Peter, of which France means to be the trusty defender."

"Well said!" exclaimed Mr. Smith. "How is it," he asked, turning to the Russian ambassador, "that you Russians are not content with your vast empire, the most extensive in the world, stretching from the banks of the Rhine to the Celestial Mountains and the Kara-Korum, whose shores are washed by the Frozen Ocean, the Atlantic, the Mediterranean, and the Indian Ocean? Then, what is the use of threats? Is war possible in view of modern inventions—asphyxiating shells capable of being projected a distance of 60 miles, an electric spark of 90 miles, that can at one stroke annihilate a battalion; to say nothing of the plague, the cholera, the yellow fever, that the belligerents might spread among their antagonists mutually, and which would in a few days destroy the greatest armies?"

"True," answered the Russian; "but can we do all that we wish? As for us Russians, pressed on our eastern frontier by the Chinese, we must at any cost put forth our strength for an effort toward the west."

"O, is that all? In that case," said Mr. Smith, "the thing can be arranged. I will speak to the Secretary of State about it. The attention of the Chinese government shall be called to the matter. This is not the first time that the Chinese have bothered us."

"Under these conditions, of course—" And the Russian ambassador declared himself satisfied.

"Ah, Sir John, what can I do for you?" asked Mr. Smith as he turned to the representative of the people of Great Britain, who till now had remained silent.

"A great deal," was the reply. "If the Earth Chronicle would but open a campaign on our behalf—"

"And for what object?"

"Simply for the annulment of the Act of Congress annexing to the United States the British islands."

Though, by a just turn-about of things here below, Great Britain has become a colony of the United States, the English are not yet reconciled to the situation. At regular intervals they are ever addressing to the American government vain complaints.

"A campaign against the annexation that has been an accomplished fact for 150 years!" exclaimed Mr. Smith. "How can your people suppose that I would do anything so unpatriotic?"

"We at home think that your people must now be sated. The Monroe doctrine is fully applied; the whole of America belongs to the Americans. What more do you want? Besides, we will pay for what we ask."

"Indeed!" answered Mr. Smith, without manifesting the slightest irritation. "Well, you English will ever be the same. No, no, Sir John, do not count on me for help. Give up our fairest province, Britain? Why not ask France generously to renounce possession of Africa, that magnificent colony the complete conquest of which cost her the labor of 800 years? You will be well received!"

"You decline! All is over then!" murmured the British agent sadly. "The United Kingdom falls to the share of the Americans; the Indies to that of—"

"The Russians," said Mr. Smith, completing the sentence.

"Australia—"

"Has an independent government."

"Then nothing at all remains for us!" sighed Sir John, downcast.

"Nothing?" asked Mr. Smith, laughing. "Well, now, there's Gibraltar!"

With this sally the audience ended. The clock was striking twelve, the hour of breakfast. Mr. Smith returns to his chamber. Where the bed stood in the morning a table all spread comes up through the floor. For Mr. Smith, being above all a practical man, has reduced the problem of existence to its simplest terms. For him, instead of the endless suites of apartments of the olden time, one room fitted with ingenious mechanical contrivances is enough. Here he sleeps, takes his meals, in short, lives.

He seats himself. In the mirror of the phonotelephote is seen the same chamber at Paris which appeared in it this morning. A table furnished forth is likewise in readiness here, for notwithstanding the difference of hours, Mr. Smith and his wife have arranged to take their meals simultaneously. It is delightful thus to take breakfast *tête-à-tête* with one who is 3000 miles or so away. Just now, Mrs. Smith's chamber has no occupant.

"She is late! Woman's punctuality! Progress everywhere except there!" muttered Mr. Smith as he turned the tap for the first dish. For like all wealthy folk in our day, Mr. Smith has done away with the domestic kitchen and is a subscriber to the Grand Alimentation Company, which sends through a great network of tubes to subscribers' residences all sorts of dishes, as a varied assortment is always in readiness. A subscription costs money, to be sure, but the *cuisine* is of the best, and the system has this advantage, that it does away with the pestering race of the *cordons-bleus*. Mr. Smith received and ate, all alone, the *hors-d'oeuvre*, *entrées*, *rôti*, and *legumes* that constituted the repast. He was just finishing the dessert when Mrs. Smith appeared in the mirror of the telephote.

"Why, where have you been?" asked Mr. Smith through the telephone.

"What! You are already at the dessert? Then I am late," she exclaimed, with a winsome *naïveté*. "Where have I been, you ask? Why, at my dress-maker's. The hats are just lovely this season! I suppose I forgot to note the time, and so am a little late."

"Yes, a little," growled Mr. Smith; "so little that I have already quite finished breakfast. Excuse me if I leave you now, but I must be going."

"O certainly, my dear; good-by till evening."

Smith stepped into his air-coach, which was in waiting for him at a window. "Where do you wish to go, sir?" inquired the coachman.

"Let me see; I have three hours," Mr. Smith mused. "Jack, take me to my accumulator works at Niagara."

For Mr. Smith has obtained a lease of the great falls of Niagara. For ages the energy developed by the falls went unutilized. Smith, applying Jackson's invention, now collects this energy, and lets or sells it. His visit to the works took more time than he had anticipated. It was four o'clock when he returned home, just in time for the daily audience which he grants to callers.

One readily understands how a man situated as Smith is must be beset with requests of all kinds. Now it is an inventor needing capital; again it is some visionary who comes to advocate a brilliant scheme which must surely yield millions of profit. A choice has to be made between these projects, rejecting the worthless, examining the questionable ones, accepting the meritorious. To this work Mr. Smith devotes every day two full hours.

The callers were fewer to-day than usual—only twelve of them. Of these, eight had only impracticable schemes to propose. In fact, one of them wanted to revive painting, an art fallen into desuetude owing to the progress made in color-photography. Another, a physician, boasted that he had discovered a cure for nasal catarrh! These impracticables were dismissed in short order. Of the four projects favorably received, the first was that of a young man whose broad forehead betokened his intellectual power.

"Sir, I am a chemist," he began, "and as such I come to you."

"Well!"

"Once the elementary bodies," said the young chemist, "were held to be sixty-two in number; a hundred years ago they were reduced to ten; now only three remain irresolvable, as you are aware."

"Yes, yes."

"Well, sir, these also I will show to be composite. In a few months, a few weeks, I shall have succeeded in solving the problem. Indeed, it may take only a few days."

"And then?"

"Then, sir, I shall simply have determined the absolute. All I want is money enough to carry my research to a successful issue."

"Very well," said Mr. Smith. "And what will be the practical outcome of your discovery?"

"The practical outcome? Why, that we shall be able to produce easily all bodies whatever—stone, wood, metal, fibers—"

"And flesh and blood?" queried Mr. Smith, interrupting him. "Do you pretend that you expect to manufacture a human being out and out?"

"Why not?"

Mr. Smith advanced $100,000 to the young chemist, and engaged his services for the Earth Chronicle laboratory.

The second of the four successful applicants, starting from experiments made so long ago as the nineteenth century and again and again repeated, had conceived the idea of removing an entire city all at once from one place to another. His special project had to do with the city of Granton, situated, as everybody knows, some fifteen miles inland. He proposes to transport the city on rails and to change it into a watering-place. The profit, of course, would be enormous. Mr. Smith, captivated by the scheme, bought a half-interest in it.

"As you are aware, sir," began applicant No. 3, "by the aid of our solar and terrestrial accumulators and transformers, we are able to make all the seasons the same. I propose to do something better still. Transform into heat a portion of the surplus energy at our disposal; send this heat to the poles; then the polar regions, relieved of their snow-cap, will become a vast territory available for man's use. What think you of the scheme?"

"Leave your plans with me, and come back in a week. I will have them examined in the meantime."

Finally, the fourth announced the early solution of a weighty scientific problem. Every one will remember the bold experiment made a hundred years ago by Dr. Nathaniel Faithburn. The doctor, being a firm believer in human hibernation—in other words, in the possibility of our suspending our vital functions and of calling them into action again after a time—resolved to subject the theory to a practical test. To this end, having first made his last will and pointed out the proper method of awakening him; having also directed that his sleep was to continue a hundred years to a day from the date of his apparent death, he unhesitatingly put the theory to the proof in his own person. Reduced to the condition of a mummy, Dr. Faithburn was coffined and laid in a tomb. Time went on. September 25th, 2889, being the day set for his resurrection, it was proposed to Mr. Smith that he should permit the second part of the experiment to be performed at his residence this evening.

"Agreed. Be here at ten o'clock," answered Mr. Smith; and with that the day's audience was closed.

Left to himself, feeling tired, he lay down on an extension chair. Then, touching a knob, he established communication with the Central Concert Hall, whence our greatest *maestros* send out to subscribers their delightful successions of accords determined by recondite algebraic formulas. Night was approaching. Entranced by the harmony, forgetful of the hour, Smith did not notice that it was growing dark. It was quite dark when he was aroused by the sound of a door opening. "Who is there?" he asked, touching a commutator.

Suddenly, in consequence of the vibrations produced, the air became luminous.

"Ah! you, Doctor?"

"Yes," was the reply. "How are you?"

"I am feeling well."

"Good! Let me see your tongue. All right! Your pulse. Regular! And your appetite?"

"Only passably good."

"Yes, the stomach. There's the rub. You are over-worked. If your stomach is out of repair, it must be mended. That requires study. We must think about it."

"In the meantime," said Mr. Smith, "you will dine with me."

As in the morning, the table rose out of the floor. Again, as in the morning, the *potage*, *rôti*, *ragoûts*, and *legumes* were supplied through the food-pipes. Toward the close of the meal, phonotelephotic communication was made with Paris. Smith saw his wife, seated alone at the dinner-table, looking anything but pleased at her loneliness.

"Pardon me, my dear, for having left you alone," he said through the telephone. "I was with Dr. Wilkins."

"Ah, the good doctor!" remarked Mrs. Smith, her countenance lighting up.

"Yes. But, pray, when are you coming home?"

"This evening."

"Very well. Do you come by tube or by air-train?"

"Oh, by tube."

"Yes; and at what hour will you arrive?"

"About eleven, I suppose."

"Eleven by Centropolis time, you mean?"

"Yes."

"Good-by, then, for a little while," said Mr. Smith as he severed communication with Paris.

Dinner over, Dr. Wilkins wished to depart. "I shall expect you at ten," said Mr. Smith. "To-day, it seems, is the day for the return to life of the famous Dr. Faithburn. You did not think of it, I suppose. The awakening is to take place here in my house. You must come and see. I shall depend on your being here."

"I will come back," answered Dr. Wilkins.

Left alone, Mr. Smith busied himself with examining his accounts—a task of vast magnitude, having to do with transactions which involve a daily expenditure of upward of $800,000. Fortunately, indeed, the stupendous progress of mechanic art in modern times makes it comparatively easy. Thanks to the Piano Electro-Reckoner, the most complex calculations can be made in a few seconds. In two hours Mr. Smith completed his task. Just in time. Scarcely had he turned over the last page when Dr. Wilkins arrived. After him came the body of Dr. Faithburn, escorted by a numerous company of men of science. They commenced work at once. The casket being laid down in the middle of the room, the telephote was got in readiness. The outer world, already notified, was anxiously expectant, for the whole world could be eye-witnesses of the performance, a reporter meanwhile, like the chorus in the ancient drama, explaining it all *viva voce* through the telephone.

"They are opening the casket," he explained. "Now they are taking Faithburn out of it—a veritable mummy, yellow, hard, and dry. Strike the body and it resounds like a block of wood. They are now applying heat; now electricity. No result. These experiments are suspended for a moment while Dr. Wilkins makes an examination of the body. Dr. Wilkins, rising, declares the man to be dead. 'Dead!' exclaims every one present. 'Yes,' answers Dr. Wilkins, 'dead!' 'And how long has he been dead?' Dr. Wilkins makes another examination. 'A hundred years,' he replies."

The case stood just as the reporter said. Faithburn was dead, quite certainly dead! "Here is a method that needs improvement," remarked Mr. Smith to Dr. Wilkins, as the scientific committee on hibernation bore the casket out. "So much for that experiment. But if poor Faithburn is dead, at least he is sleeping," he continued. "I wish I could get some sleep. I am tired out, Doctor, quite tired out! Do you not think that a bath would refresh me?"

"Certainly. But you must wrap yourself up well before you go out into the hall-way. You must not expose yourself to cold."

"Hall-way? Why, Doctor, as you well know, everything is done by machinery here. It is not for me to go to the bath; the bath will come to me. Just look!" and he pressed a button. After a few seconds a faint rumbling was heard, which grew louder and louder. Suddenly the door opened, and the tub appeared.

Such, for this year of grace 2889, is the history of one day in the life of the editor of the Earth Chronicle. And the history of that one day is the history of 365 days every year, except leap-years, and then of 366 days—for as yet no means has been found of increasing the length of the terrestrial year.

Jules Verne

A Note About the Author

Jules Verne (1828–1905) was a French novelist, poet and playwright. Verne is considered a major French and European author, as he has a wide influence on avant-garde and surrealist literary movements, and is also credited as one of the primary inspirations for the steampunk genre. However, his influence does not stop in the literary sphere. Verne's work has also provided invaluable impact on scientific fields as well. Verne is best known for his series of bestselling adventure novels, which earned him such an immense popularity that he is one of the world's most translated authors.

Michel Verne (1861–1925) was a French writer, editor and son of the famed science fiction author, Jules Verne. Though the two shared a difficult relationship, especially during Michel's adolescence, Michel was responsible for publishing many of his father's final works. He often collaborated with his father around this time, editing and expanding the narratives of notable Jules Verne titles, such as *In the Year 2889*, *The Eternal Adam*, and *Survivors of the Johnathan*. Though his own work displayed promise, Michel nearly exclusively published under his father's name, upholding the literary legacy of Jules Verne posthumously.

A Note from the Publisher

Spanning many genres, from non-fiction essays to literature classics to children's books and lyric poetry, Mint Edition books showcase the master works of our time in a modern new package. The text is freshly typeset, is clean and easy to read, and features a new note about the author in each volume. Many books also include exclusive new introductory material. Every book boasts a striking new cover, which makes it as appropriate for collecting as it is for gift giving. Mint Edition books are only printed when a reader orders them, so natural resources are not wasted. We're proud that our books are never manufactured in excess and exist only in the exact quantity they need to be read and enjoyed.

Discover more of your favorite classics with Bookfinity™.

- Track your reading with custom book lists.
- Get great book recommendations for your personalized Reader Type.
- Add reviews for your favorite books.
- AND MUCH MORE!

Visit **bookfinity.com** and take the fun Reader Type quiz to get started.

Enjoy our classic and modern companion pairings!